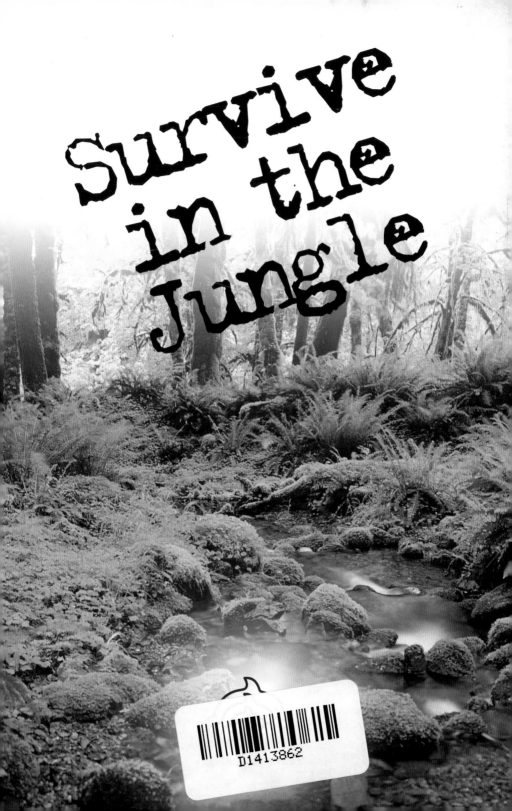

Survive in the Jungle

Silver Dolphin Books
An imprint of the Advantage Publishers Group
5880 Oberlin Drive, San Diego, CA 92121-4794
www.silverdolphinbooks.com

WARNING!

This book provides useful information for difficult situations an individual may encounter, but it cannot guarantee results, nor can the publisher accept any responsibility for any injuries, damages, or loss resulting from the information within this book. The red WARNING symbol shown above denotes situations or activities that require caution. Never put yourself in danger and always seek the advice of an adult before trying any of the activities in this book, especially those highlighted with a WARNING symbol.

Created and produced by
Andromeda Children's Books
An imprint of Pinwheel Ltd
Winchester House
259-269 Old Marylebone Road
London NW1 5XJ, United Kingdom
www.pinwheel.co.uk

ISBN 1-59223-431-3

1 2 3 4 5   09 08 07 06 05
Made in China

Author Claire Llewellyn
Managing Editor Ruth Hooper
Series Editor Deborah Murrell, **Assitant Editor** Emily Hawkins
Art Director Ali Scrivens, **Art Editor** Julia Harris, **Designer** Miranda Kennedy
Production Clive Sparling, **Illustrator** Peter Bull

Contents

Introduction

You are lost in the jungle!
All you have with you is a backpack with a
few useful things inside. It will be 12 days
before help can arrive.

Can you survive on your own?

Can you find fresh water and food?

Can you deal with jungle creatures?

Could you make use of the things in your backpack?

Here is the survival challenge!
On each page of this book, you face a different challenge.
The 12 challenges explore every aspect of life in the jungle—
from building a shelter and finding food and water to
making your way out of the thick vegetation to open
ground, where you can be seen and rescued.

What's in your backpack

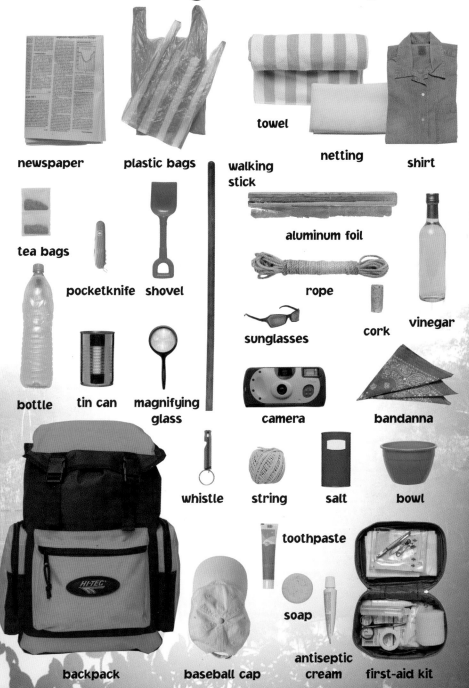

newspaper

plastic bags

walking stick

towel

netting

shirt

tea bags

pocketknife

shovel

aluminum foil

rope

sunglasses

cork

vinegar

bottle

tin can

magnifying glass

camera

bandanna

whistle

string

salt

bowl

toothpaste

soap

backpack

baseball cap

antiseptic cream

first-aid kit

Could you make a shelter?

A tropical jungle can be an uncomfortably hot, wet environment. You will need to build a shelter—a safe, dry place to rest and sleep. Use the natural materials around you to build the shelter. Get started early in the day, and try to be methodical and careful. You don't want to have to do it all over again in pouring rain, or the middle of the night!

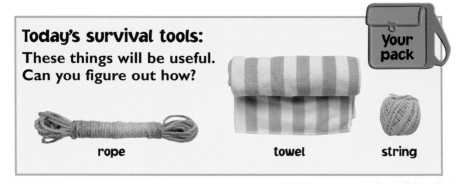

Today's survival tools:
These things will be useful. Can you figure out how?

your pack

rope

towel

string

Where is the best place to set up camp?

It is best to build your shelter close to a river. It will be a source of food and water, a place to wash, and a vital transportation route. Look for a patch of raised, level ground, which is unlikely to flood and where the vegetation can be easily cleared. If you can, find well-spaced trees so you can build a shelter between them.

Shelter
Tips

1. Check that there are no coconuts or dead wood above your shelter. They could crash down on you.

2. Avoid places with lots of dead wood and leaf mold on the ground—they harbor insects, scorpions, and centipedes.

3. If you run out of rope, use vines or young green saplings.

4. String a rope or vine between two trees so you can hang up your clothes and boots to dry.

What do you need to build a shelter?

1. You will need a branch or a piece of bamboo long enough to stretch between the two trees, and several more about 6 feet long. You will also need large leaves and long, strong vines.

2. If the two trees have natural forks to rest the long branch on, use these. If not, lash it to the trunks using a bowline knot (see below).

3. Lean the other branches against this to form A-shapes for the walls, lashing the tops together securely with vines.

4. Using a sharp stick, make holes close to the stems of the leaves. Thread the leaves together in rows with the string or vines to make a large sheet. Make sure that the upper leaves overlap the lower ones.

5. Attach the leaf sheet to the long support with more string and repeat for the other side. You now have two waterproof walls!

6. Attach a row of leaves lengthwise along the top of the two sheets to cover the gap where the leaf sheets meet.

Jungle bugs   ○ Facts!

The jungle is crawling with insects. Scientists estimate that about 50 million different kinds live in tropical jungles. An average of 600 different insects live on each and every tree!

Where will you sleep?

It's important that you get a good night's sleep so you can face the challenges ahead. The jungle floor is very damp, so you will need to sleep off the ground. You can use your large towel as a hammock by lashing it between two trees with rope or vines. Make sure you test it for safety before jumping in!

Tying a bowline knot

Try it at home!

A bowline is simple to learn. It is also quick and secure, and will not slip.

1. Wind some rope around a tree. Make a small loop in the rope and bring the end up through it.

2. Wind the end around the main part of the rope and bring it back down through the loop.

3. Pull the loose end and the main rope to tighten the knot.

Can you find fresh water?

USE CAUTIO

Once you have built your shelter, your next task is to find clean drinking water—your body cannot do without it. Fortunately, water is easy to find in the jungle, but can you be sure it is clean?

Today's survival tools:
These things will be useful. Can you figure out how?

Your pack

bowl   salt   shirt   string

Why is water so important?

Every day, your body needs about 8 cups of water. In the jungle, it will need much more, because you will sweat a lot in the humid conditions. To replace the water you lose, try to drink about 20 cups a day. Your body also needs salt—about half a tablespoon a day. You lose it when you sweat, and it is vital to replace it. Each time you take a drink, add a tiny pinch of salt to the water.

Collecting water

Q and **A**

Q: How can I collect water?

A: Collect water in a clean container. Look for running water, and collect it as close to its source (such as a spring or waterfall) as possible.

Q: Where can I find water when I'm on the move?

A: Some plants are perfectly shaped to catch rainwater. But don't forget to strain out any insects first!

Q: Can I use water from the river?

A: A fast-flowing stream with a stony or sandy bed will be much cleaner than a slow-moving river.

Can you collect rainwater?

Rain falls regularly in the jungle. Set up plenty of rain traps, using the biggest leaves you can find to funnel water into containers such as bamboo cups.

Can you make use of plants?

Types of jungle

○ Facts!

"Primary" jungle has both tall trees and smaller plants. When people clear an area for crops and then abandon it, the undergrowth and creepers are the first to grow back. This "secondary" jungle is denser and more difficult to travel through.

You can find water inside some jungle plants. Look for a stem of green bamboo, then bend it over toward the ground and tie it down over a container. Cut off the top of the stem and water will drip out. Banana plants are a good source of water. Cut the top off a plant about 2 feet above the ground and scoop out the middle of the stump. This will slowly fill with water that flows up from the roots.

How can you make your water safe?

Even water that looks clean may contain harmful bacteria—tiny living things that can cause disease. The best way to kill the bacteria is to boil the water for at least 10 minutes. If you have no way of boiling water, filtering it will remove many impurities.

① Push three sticks firmly into the ground so that they form a triangle. Make sure they are at least six inches deep in the ground.

② Tie a knot in the end of a shirt sleeve and fill it with layers of crumbled charcoal, then sand, and finally grass.

③ Place the shirt on the frame so that the sleeve hangs in the center. Tie it onto the sticks securely with string.

④ Put a container underneath the end of the sleeve and pour water through the filter. You should end up with clear, drinkable water!

Can you handle the humidity?

It is your third day and the climate is getting to you. It's hot and sticky, and the daily downpours mean your clothes are always damp. Today's challenge is to find ways of handling the humidity.

Today's survival tools:

These things will be useful. Can you figure out how?

bandanna

newspaper

plastic bags

Your pack

salt

You are feeling exhausted. How can you cope?

The jungle climate is clammy and hot, and any kind of effort is exhausting. Change your daily routine: get your tasks out of the way early by rising at dawn, working until noon, then resting during the hottest part of the day. While you work, you will have to pace yourself. Don't feel guilty about taking plenty of rest breaks: they will help you conserve your energy.

Can you cope with the rain?

There will be heavy downpours every day, usually in the afternoon. Always try to seek shelter. If you are caught in the rain, take a tip from the orangutans in the jungles of Southeast Asia—use large leaves as natural umbrellas.

Staying cool — Tips

1. Wear loose clothing.
2. Cool your head with a damp bandanna.
3. Drink plenty of water with a pinch of salt.
4. Fan yourself with a large leaf.
5. Plunge your wrists in cold water when you need to cool off.

How can you dry off?

In the jungle you are likely to be wet most of the time. It's best to have a set of "wet" clothes and a set of "dry" clothes. Keep your dry clothes dry by storing them in the plastic bags you have in your backpack. Every evening, after a wash, put on your dry clothes. This will boost your morale and keep you warm. Wash your wet clothes and hang them up to drip, and put them on again in the morning. Don't forget to air your boots. Prop them on sticks or hang them on a clothesline. Stuff them with the newspaper from your backpack. It will help to absorb the water.

Climate

Q and A

Q: Why are jungles so hot and wet?

A: Jungles lie near the equator, where it is always hot. Every morning, the sun heats the ground, drawing water from the soil and changing it into a gas called water vapor. This warm gas rises, cools, and becomes clouds, which soon lead to rain.

Q: What is humidity?

A: Humidity is the amount of water vapor in the air. In a desert, the humidity is less than 10 percent. In a jungle, it can be as much as 88 percent! It is hard for the body to cool down because there is already so much water in the air that our sweat cannot evaporate.

How will you take care of your body?

The warm, damp climate makes your body sweat, providing perfect conditions for bacteria to spread. It's important to wash properly every day. Pay special attention to your feet, where fungus can take hold. Dry them well and try to keep them dry. Take care of your teeth by brushing them with a stick dipped in the charcoal, or charred wood, that remains after a fire (see page 20). Charcoal attracts impurities and gets rid of unpleasant flavors and smells. Your teeth may be black, but at least they'll be clean!

Cooling down—fast!

Try it at home!

When you are feeling overheated, plunge your wrists in cold water. This is a quick way to cool down. How does it work? When your body is hot, blood vessels near the wrist enlarge, or expand, to give off heat. In cold water, this is quickly released, and cooler blood flows around the body, helping to cool you down.

How will you explore the jungle?

DAY 4

Food is running low, so you will need to find supplies in the wild. You are surrounded by plants and animals, but which of them are good and safe to eat? Searching for food takes a lot of effort. This is no time to be squeamish!

Today's survival tools:
These things will be useful.
Can you figure out how?

Your pack

walking stick   string   bandages

What is the best way to get through the jungle?

In a jungle, the plants grow so closely together that they create an almost impenetrable wall. It is possible to hack a path with a stick, but this is slow and exhausting. Before you try, take time to look around: sometimes you can spot a trail that other people or animals have made. There may also be natural trails, such as riverbanks. Using a trail will certainly be quicker than hacking a path through the jungle. But remember, wild animals use these trails too, so always be alert to danger!

Jungle science

Facts!

Local people have been using jungle plants as medicines for many generations. Scientists have only recently begun to discover how the medicines work.

Scientists have recorded over 300 different kinds of trees in a 2½-acre area of a jungle.

Jungle plants

Q: Why does everything grow so well in a jungle?

A: Jungles are natural greenhouses; their warmth and humidity are perfect for plants, which grow and grow!

Q: Why do some plants grow off the ground?

A: Some jungle plants, known as epiphytes, perch high up in the branches of trees. They get more light here than they would on the ground. Their roots don't reach the ground, so they take in water from the air.

Which plants will cause the most difficulty?

Some jungle plants have vicious defenses to keep animals from eating them. Many vines have spikes or sharp cutting edges that can shred your clothing and slash your skin. If you get tangled up in something like this, don't try to battle against it. Move backward so that the vine releases you and then find another way through. Jungle explorers carry a machete, a tool with a heavy blade that is used to hack away vines, make clearings, and chop poles for building. The machete is highly dangerous. It is used with a slashing action, which is hard to control.

How can you protect your skin?

In the undergrowth, skin will get scratched and stung—so, in spite of the heat, always keep yourself covered. If you have them, wear a hat with a brim, strong boots, long pants, and a closely woven long-sleeved cotton shirt. If your hands get cut, clean and cover the wounds with a bandage, otherwise they will become infected. It's always best to carry a strong stick, which you can use to push branches aside. It may also be useful as a walking stick and, if necessary, to ward off attacking animals.

What if you get lost?

Poor visibility and thick vegetation make it easy to lose your sense of direction even on short trips. Until you are familiar with the area, use the string in your backpack to make a trail to help you return to your shelter. If you go farther than the string will reach, mark a trail with sticks or piles of stones on the ground.

Make a trail

Try it at home!

Next time you're in a park or the country, go for a walk with an adult. Leave arrows made of sticks pointing the way back to help you retrace your steps.

Can you cope with bugs?

Insects and other pests flourish in jungles because there is a constant supply of food. You'll find them everywhere—in your shelter, clothes, and backpack, and on your arms and legs. Some of them bite and spread disease. How can you keep them away?

Today's survival tools:
These things will be useful. Can you figure out how?

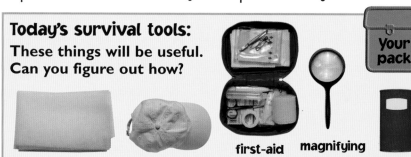

Your pack

netting | baseball cap | first-aid kit | magnifying glass | salt

Can you protect yourself from mosquitoes?

Mosquitoes will try to feed on your blood. Their mouthparts are shaped like tiny tubes, which they use to reach into blood capillaries under your skin. They carry bacteria that can cause disease. Mosquitoes are plentiful after dusk, so you must cover up. Tuck your pants into your socks. Wear a long-sleeved shirt and keep your hands covered. Make a head net from the netting in your backpack (see opposite). When you go to bed, smear mud on your face to form a hard surface that mosquitoes cannot pierce.

Insects
Tips

1. Keep away from low, swampy ground, which is home to mosquitoes and leeches.

2. Avoid scented soap: it attracts insects.

3. Do not disturb wasp, bee, or hornet nests. They may attack.

4. Try not to scratch mosquito bites. If you do, they are likely to get infected and could make you really ill.

14

How can you avoid ants?

The jungle floor is teeming with ants. Many of them give painful stings, particularly driver ants. Never sit on the jungle floor. Make a bench at your shelter site using strong saplings or bamboo canes lashed together with rope or vines. Spread ash around the site to deter ants.

Make a head net

Try it at home!

1. Find a large piece of netting, such as an old fishing net or drape.

2. Put on an old baseball cap. Wearing the cap, place the netting over your head. The cap keeps the netting away from your skin so that insects cannot bite you.

3. Tuck all the ends inside your shirt.

A head net like this will help to protect you from all kinds of insects.

Can you remove ticks and leeches?

Ticks and leeches like nothing better than to stick to your skin and suck out your blood. Never try to pull them off—their mouthparts will break off and cause infection under the skin. To remove a leech or tick, sprinkle it with salt to make it release its grip, then pull it off using tweezers. Ticks are tiny, so a magnifying glass will help you see them.

Which foods are safe?

USE CAUTION

Your food supplies are running low. There are plenty of plants available in the jungle, but which of them are good to eat? Some safe foods may be strange or off-putting. Can you face eating them?

Today's survival tools:

Your pack

These things will be useful. Can you figure out how?

tin can   salt

Why do you need food?

Food gives us energy. If you run short of food in the jungle, you will simply run out of energy. Then everyday tasks, such as lighting a fire, will become almost impossible. Even worse, without energy you'll be unable to concentrate, make decisions, or use tools safely.

Which foods will give me the most energy?

The most energy-rich foods are edible roots, fruits, nuts, and seeds. Only eat foods that you recognize, such as Brazil nuts and coconuts. Nuts are especially useful because you can pick plenty and carry them around with you for a quick, energy-boosting snack.

Food

Tips

1. The farther you travel to look for food, the more you need to eat to keep your energy level up. Save energy by looking for food close by.

2. Use a long stick to "fish" for ants and termites in their nests.

3. Don't gather more than you need. Food spoils quickly in the jungle heat and can attract unwelcome animals.

4. Never eat something if you are not sure what it is or if you are not sure that it is safe.

Which animals are safe?

Insects are easy to trap (see below) and contain up to 80 percent protein. You can add them to soups. Snails can also be eaten. Before cooking them, stir salt into clean water and leave the snails to soak for a couple of days to clean out their systems in case they have eaten poisonous plants.

Safe animals

- Ants
- Butterflies
- Fish
- Grasshoppers and crickets
- Snails (unless brightly colored)
- Frogs (unless brightly colored)
- Grubs
- Worms
- Birds' eggs

Unsafe animals

- Biting or stinging insects
- Toads and brightly colored frogs
- Hairy or brightly colored insects
- Spiders, mosquitoes, and ticks

Safe plants

- Bananas
- Papayas
- Mangoes
- Figs
- Palm hearts
- Bamboo shoots
- Palm shoots

Unsafe plants

- Mushrooms and other fungi
- Plants with a three-leaved growth pattern
- Beans, bulbs, or seeds from pods
- Grain heads with pink, purple, or black spurs

Where should you look for plants?

Different plants grow in different areas. Look in water for water lilies, whose roots are edible, and further inland for fruit trees. Some parts of the jungle may have been cleared for farming and then abandoned, so keep your eyes open for any surviving food plants. Jungle fruits, such as bananas, are a delicious source of vitamins.

Make an insect trap

1. Put a tin can in a hole in the ground so that its top is at ground level.
2. Cover it with a piece of wood balanced on top of two stones.
3. Insects will seek shade under the wood and fall into the trap.

Try it at home!

Can you fish in the river?

DAY 7

Jungles are crisscrossed by rivers and streams, which contain fish and other tasty creatures. But catching them will be a real challenge. Be patient and you will be rewarded with a fresh fish for dinner!

Today's survival tools:

These things will be useful. Can you figure out how?

Your pack

cork

| netting | pocketknife | first-aid kit | plastic bottle | string |

Can you make a fishing line?

Cut a strong, straight sapling long enough to use as a fishing rod. Tie the string from your backpack to one end. Tie a safety pin to the end of the line and open the pin to make a hook. Fish feed at different depths: some snap at flies at the surface; others feed on vegetation on the riverbed. Your fishing line will naturally sink to deeper water. To make it float, tie on the cork.

What is good bait?

If possible, use creatures that live in or near the water as bait for your fishing line: insects, grubs, worms, and shellfish. These are your prey's usual diet, and will tempt it to bite.

Piranhas

Facts!

Piranhas are some of the fiercest freshwater fish in the world. They have powerful jaws and very sharp teeth.

Piranhas like to feed on live prey. They will bite the fins and flesh of other fish that get too close.

Are little fish a waste of time?

In some ways, little fish are better than large ones. If the fish you catch is more than 2 inches long (about a thumb's length), you will need to gut it (remove its internal organs) before eating it. But if it is less than 2 inches, you can eat it whole. So if you're squeamish, it's best to throw back larger fish. If you have a plastic bottle, you can make a simple trap for catching small fish (see below).

Can you find other river foods?

Shellfish, such as shrimp, can be easily collected in most freshwater streams. Use the netting from your backpack. Flush out the shrimp by disturbing the leaves at the bottom of the stream. Then scoop the shrimp up in your net a little way downstream. You may also find some freshwater mussels—look for old shells washed up on the banks, and search below the waterline for live ones.

Make a bottle trap

Try it at home!

1. Cut the bottle off just below the neck.

2. Push the neck backward into the bottle.

3. Make a small hole near the open end and tie the trap to something to keep it in place.

4. Place the trap in water, making sure it fills with water. Fish can easily swim in, but will often be unable to get out again.

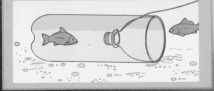

Can fish injure you?

Some freshwater fish can cause nasty injuries. Catfish have sharp spines on their fins, and their skin is covered with a poisonous slime. These are defenses the fish has evolved that help it avoid predators. If you grab a catfish, it could cut you and give you a nasty rash. Also, if you don't want to be stung, avoid freshwater stingrays! Although piranhas are fierce, they are only likely to attack you if there is no smaller prey around. But if you catch and land a piranha, watch out for its sharp teeth!

What do you know about fire?

DAY 8

Fire has many uses in addition to cooking. It can be used to keep you and your clothes dry and warm, to keep insects away, and to signal for help. Making a fire is dangerous, but it is a vital survival skill.

USE CAUTION

WARNING

It is useful to know how to build a fire, but you should never try to make a fire on your own. Always have adult supervision. When learning how to build a fire, you should remember these important things.

What should be used as fuel?

Tinder is something that will catch fire easily, so you can use it to start a fire. Dry grass, fluffy seeds, and even cotton balls make really good tinder. To get the fire burning, you will need kindling, like long, fine twigs or dried leaves. To keep a campfire going, you will need to find wood—preferably dead wood that has not fallen onto damp ground. Standing trees, dead or alive, are home to birds and insects, so leave them intact.

Use small pieces of wood—no larger than the diameter of an adult wrist—that can be broken with your hands. This practice avoids having to use a saw or hatchet and the wood will readily burn to ash.

Where is a good spot for a fire?

You should find an area away from your shelter where wood is plentiful. Stay away from anything that can catch fire accidentally, like bushes or undergrowth, and keep wood and other sources of fuel away from the fire. Fires should be built on sand or soil and you should have water, sand, or loose dirt at hand, ready to put out the fire. Never leave a fire unattended and be sure to thoroughly extinguish all fires: when you're ready to stop using the fire, stop adding new wood and instead toss in burned ends of wood. Allow the wood to burn to white ash, thoroughly soak with water, and cover it with sand and dirt.

Fire **Q and A**

Q: Where is the best place to find firewood?

A: Look for dry, dead wood caught in the branches of trees.

Q: What if it is too windy to light a fire?

A: Make your campfire in a sheltered area, or dig a shallow trench.

Q: Is a bigger campfire always better?

A: No—big fires need a lot of fuel and their heat is often wasted.

⚠ USE CAUTION

WARNING
Never try to make a fire on your own. Always have adult supervision.

Are animals dangerous?

DAY 9

Jungles are home to a huge variety of animals, and some of them are dangerous. Most would rather keep out of your way, but if they are hungry or protecting their young, they could be a real threat. Can you avoid potential danger and keep yourself safe?

Today's survival tools:
These things will be useful.
Can you figure out how?

Your pack

walking stick   plastic bags   sunglasses

Snakes   **Tips**

1. Never walk barefooted.

2. Turn your boots upside down before you put them on.

3. Never put your hand where you can't see.

4. Never climb trees that have thick leaves.

5. Never swim in muddy water.

Which snakes live in jungles?

Many snakes live in jungles. The anaconda lives in rivers and swamps, and kills by wrapping itself around its prey tightly, until it can no longer breathe. Other snakes, such as vipers, have a deadly venom. Some snakes spray venom into animals' eyes. Wearing sunglasses will help to protect you from these. Always be on the lookout for snakes. If you see one, back away slowly.

How are frogs dangerous?

Some frogs are poisonous. Poison-arrow frogs have highly toxic skin, which some jungle tribes use to poison their arrows. Luckily, these frogs are easy to spot: they are small and black with bright splashes of red, green, blue, or yellow. If you ever need to move a poison-arrow frog, use a plastic bag from your backpack as a protective glove.

Could you escape from a big cat?

Leopards, tigers, jaguars, and panthers all live in tropical jungles. They hunt mostly at night, so you should be safe during the day. If you see one, don't run away; stand up tall, stare into its eyes, and slowly back away. Cats rarely attack humans unless they feel threatened. Never bend over to pick up a stone to throw; you will look like a four-legged animal and the cat may attack. If it does, fight back as hard as you can. Take care to protect your throat, where the cat will try to bite.

Could you ward off an alligator?

Both alligators and crocodiles live in jungles. They may be aggressive when they have eggs or young, and often shelter in shallow burrows along riverbanks when guarding a nearby nest. If you see one, freeze and then slowly back away. If it attacks, use your stick to hit it on the head, especially the nostrils and ears. Smaller members of the crocodile family, such as gharials and caymans, also live in jungles.

Can you care for yourself?

DAY 10

You have been living in the jungle for over a week and are beginning to feel the strain. This is the time when it's easy to have an accident or succumb to an infection. If you are injured or feel unwell, can you look after yourself?

Today's survival tools:

These things will be useful. Can you figure out how?

Your pack

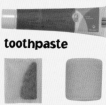

toothpaste

shovel | salt | soap | green tea bag | gauze | vinegar | antiseptic cream

What should you do with bites and stings?

Bites can quickly cause infection. It's important to treat them with care. If you are stung by a bee, remove the stinger, then wash the area with vinegar. This works as an antidote to the sting. Wash insect bites with soap and apply an antiseptic cream. If you are bitten by a leech, squeeze the wound to make sure it is clean. When it stops bleeding, a blood clot will form.

First aid

Q and A

Q: How can I stop my bites from itching?

A: Apply a dab of toothpaste. This will help stop the itching and also acts as an antiseptic, preventing infection.

Q: Should I suck the poison out of a snakebite?

A: Never try to suck poison out of a bite. Your body could absorb it through the lining of your mouth, and you could end up spreading the poison around your body.

How do you treat a scald?

You have scalded your hand while boiling water. Quickly put it under cold water, preferably running water, and hold it there for about 10 minutes. Now dry your hand gently and dress it with gauze to keep infections from entering the wound. Use the green tea bags in your backpack to make some tea. Bathe your hand regularly in the cooled tea; it encourages burns to heal.

How do you heal a cut?

If you cut yourself, press the edges of the wound together—in time it will begin to seal. If the wound continues to bleed, press hard with a pad until the bleeding stops. Put a clean pad on the wound and bandage it in place. Change the bandage daily to avoid infection.

Snakes
○ **Facts!**

Not all snakes bite. Some constrict, or squeeze, their prey to death. Others spray venom rather than injecting it by biting. Even if you have been bitten by a poisonous snake, it may not have injected poison. If it has, the area of the bite swells almost immediately.

How do you treat a snakebite?

1. Wash the wound thoroughly to get rid of germs.
2. Dry it gently and cover it with a bandage. Change it daily to keep the wound clean.
3. Wrap a compressional knot above the bite and keep the area as still as you can, or put it in a splint. Rest as much as possible while your body fights the poison.

You think you've eaten something poisonous. What should you do?

The best thing to do, however unpleasant it may be, is to make yourself vomit. Vomiting will dehydrate you, so drink plenty of water with a pinch of salt. Some ginger root tea will make you feel better. Ginger grows wild in the jungle. Dig up a root, peel the skin, and boil it in water for about five minutes. Sip the tea slowly.

Can you find a way out?

Your survival challenge is drawing to a close. It's time to pack up, leave your shelter, and try to get out of the jungle. Can you find a way out of the jungle into the open, where you can be seen and rescued?

Today's survival tools:
These things will be useful. Can you figure out how?

Your pack

rope   walking stick

Can you travel on foot?

Traveling on foot won't be easy in the dense vegetation of the jungle. It is worst in places where trees have fallen or been cut down, and new plants have grown up thickly. Can you climb up to a ridge where there is less vegetation, or find a well-worn track, perhaps along a stream? If you do have to travel through dense jungle, take care not to disturb snakes or insects; use your stick to move plants aside.

Walking   **Tips**

1. Start walking early. Rest in the shade when it is hot.

2. Don't hurry. Try to maintain a steady pace, and take regular rests to avoid fatigue.

3. Carry plenty of clean drinking water, in case you don't find any along the way.

4. Don't walk beneath dead trees; they could fall and injure you.

5. Steer clear of muddy swamps. They are home to mosquitoes, leeches, crocodiles, and snakes.

Can you travel by river?

You have found a wide, slow river. Villages are usually found on the banks of a river. Using your watch as a compass (see below), you determine that this river is flowing south. You think you have spotted a village to the south. Can you construct a bamboo raft and float downstream toward it?

(1) Cut about 20 strong bamboo stems about 10 feet long and arrange them in a double layer.

(2) Make holes in the sides of the stems and thread your rope or a long stick through them to fasten them together.

(3) Lash the structure tightly together with rope or long vines.

(4) Now tie your raft to a rock or tree and test it in shallow water. Does it float? Step carefully onto it to make sure that it will float with your weight on it.

Use your watch as a compass

In the Northern Hemisphere (north of the equator), hold your watch so that the hour hand points to the sun. South is about halfway between the 12 and the hour hand.

In the Southern Hemisphere (south of the equator), hold your watch so that the 12 points to the sun. North is about halfway between the 12 and the hour hand.

Try it at home!

Can you stay safe on the river?

Before you wade into the river, tuck your pants into your socks to keep leeches out. Watch for piranhas, crocodiles, and other predators, and do not enter the water if you spot any. If you do enter the water, use a strong stick for support. Stay away from rocks, very deep water, and strong currents.

Rafting

Tips

1. Build your raft close to the river.

2. Make a paddle by tying several sticks together with vines.

3. Tie loose items to your raft for safety. You don't want to lose them.

4. Avoid collisions, which could break your raft.

Can you find help?

Congratulations! You have survived for 11 days in the jungle and have overcome many challenges, including finding your way out. Today you face your final challenge: can you find someone to help you?

Today's survival tools:
These things will be useful. Can you figure out how?

whistle

Your pack

aluminum foil

camera

Can you find people to help you?

Although the jungle seems uninhabited, it is home to many groups of people. They can help you on your onward journey. Many communities live in villages on the river. Look for signs of human activity, such as tracks, bridges, or wisps of smoke. Listen for the sound of voices or boat engines. If you hear anything in the distance, blow hard on the whistle from your backpack. If there is anyone there, they will come and find you.

Can you make yourself be seen?

A search-and-rescue helicopter is looking for you, but it's going to be hard for the pilot to spot you under the canopy of trees. You need to make yourself more visible from the air. The only place where there is open sky is directly above the river, and this is the place where the helicopter will look. Tether your raft to a rock or tree on the bank and use it as a platform from which to signal.

Can you make signals?

Search and rescue pilots notice anything out of the ordinary. Can you attract their attention? If it's sunny and you hear the helicopter, try to flash signals by reflecting the sunlight:

1. Get a flat stone and wrap it in the aluminum foil from your backpack.

2. Tilt the shiny surface in the direction of the sun until a flash is reflected on the ground.

3. Move the flash up toward the helicopter, then down again.

4. After the sun has dipped below the trees and it is dark, you can signal with your camera flash instead.

Helicopter rescue

Q: Where will the helicopter land?

A: There may not be anywhere for the pilot to land. In this case, the helicopter will hover in midair while a second person is lowered to rescue you.

Q: Should I make any special preparations?

A: Helicopter rotor blades create strong winds. Clear the rescue site of anything that could be blown around in the wind, making it hard to see.

Flash a signal

Use the instructions above to make flash signals. Instead of a stone wrapped in aluminum foil, you could use a small hand mirror. Try to control the flash by moving it up and down.

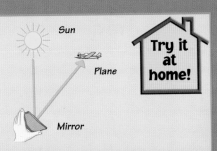

Sun

Plane

Mirror

Try it at home!

So you think you could survive?

How much have you learned about survival in the jungle? Can you answer these questions correctly? All the information can be found in the book. After taking the quiz, check your answers on page 32.

1. Where is the best place to build your shelter?

a. In a banana tree

b. On raised level ground close to a river or stream

c. Near a swamp

2. How much water will you need each day?

a. 2 cups

b. 20 cups

c. 200 cups

3. Which of these can you use to clean your teeth?

a. A stick dipped in charcoal

b. Soap

c. Dry leaves

4. Why shouldn't you sleep on the jungle floor?

a. Because the ground could shake

b. Because it is dark

c. Because it is always damp

5. What is the best way to remove a leech?

a. By pulling it off

b. By putting it under water for a few minutes

c. By sprinkling it with salt

6. Which of these foods are not safe to eat?

a. Mushrooms

b. Bananas

c. Bamboo shoots

7. Which freshwater fish is the fiercest?

a. Catfish

b. Piranha

c. Stingray

8. Which of these make good tinder for a fire?

a. Fluffy seeds

b. Small stones

c. Banana leaves

9. Why should you not touch a brightly colored frog?

a. Because it could bite you

b. Because it is endangered

c. Because its skin could be toxic

10. You've been badly bitten by insects. What should you do?

a. Wash the bites with soap and apply antiseptic cream

b. Lie down in the shade and fan yourself

c. Suck the bites and put vinegar on them

11. What is a good way to find a village in the jungle?

a. Follow a river

b. Climb a tree

c. Walk around in circles

12. What can you use as a compass?

a. The wind direction

b. A small stone

c. Your watch

13. Where is a good place for a helicopter to spot you?

a. Under the jungle canopy

b. On a raft in the middle of the river

c. On a track made by animals

14. Which is the the best signal to use at night?

a. A camera flash

b. A smoky fire

c. A ground-to-air message

---

now check your answers with those on page 32.
How many did you answer correctly?

12–14 correct answers:

Congratulations; you're a true survivor!

9–11 correct answers:

Pretty good; you'd probably make it through!

4–8 correct answers:

You might be lucky and survive, but you could probably do with learning some more skills!

1–3 correct answers:

Try not to get stranded in a jungle—or brush up on your survival skills first!

Index

Picture credits: All images supplied by Corbis. 2–3 Gavriel Jecan; 4–5 Ann Johansson; 6–7 Morton Beebe, 8–9 Hubert Stadler; 10–11 Danny Lehman; 12–13 Gavriel Jecan; 14–15 Wolfgang Kaehler; 16–17 Bernardo Bucci; 18–19 Martin Harvey, Gallo Images; 20–21 Doug Wilson; 22–23 George D. Lepp; 24–25, 26–27 Gary Braasch; 28–29 Neil Robinowitz; 32 Sergio Pitamitz.

Answers to quiz on pages 30–31:

1. b, **2**. b, **3**. a, **4**. c, **5**. c, **6**. a, **7**. b, **8**. a, **9**. c, **10**. a, **11**. a, **12**. c, **13**. b, **14**. a